There's a Worm in My Apple

SHEENA BAKER

ILLUSTRATED BY

LYNN JOHNSTON

First published in 1985 by Stoddart Publishing
A Division of General Publishing Co. Limited
30 Lesmill Road, Toronto, Ontario M3B 2T6

CANADIAN CATALOGUING IN PUBLICATION DATA

Baker, Sheena
   There's a worm in my apple

ISBN 0-7737-5029-0.

1. Elementary school teaching — Anecdotes,
facetiae, satire, etc. 2. Elementary school
teaching — Caricatures and cartoons.
3. Canadian wit and humor (English)*
4. Canadian wit and humor, Pictorial.*
I. Johnston, Lynn, 1947- . II. Title.

LA23.B34 1985   372.11'002'07   C85-098149-2

0-7737-5029-0
Printed and bound in Canada

Second printing, December, 1985.

Introduction

Virtually ever teacher at one time or another has said, "How I wish I had kept a diary of all the funny things that have happened over the years!" This is especially true of the elementary teacher.

I'm an elementary teacher who has been in the education game for some twenty years. Like everyone else, I've been sorry that I didn't record the pearls of wit and wisdom that I've heard from the lips of young children.

When Lynn Johnston came to see me about the classroom antics of her young son, I relieved her motherly insecurity by describing some of the things my other students had done over the years. She responded by challenging me to write a book — which she, in turn, promised to illustrate. I was very doubtful that I could do it. A couple of days after her suggestion, I had an hour to spare and I sat and jotted down a few memories. To my amazement, I had over a hundred ideas down on paper.

This book grew from that beginning. I've enjoyed writing it. Recalling incidents from the past has given me almost as much pleasure as experiencing them over the years. If you have young children, teach young children, or just plain *like* young children, I hope you'll get a laugh or two as you turn the pages.

Kindergarten

Of Coathangers and Clothing

Every parent who's gone through the experience knows how emotionally wrenching it is to leave their children on that first day of kindergarten. Think how the poor child feels! There he is, being left by himself in a big room with a big adult and seventeen little strangers.

To make matters worse, the child senses that mom is upset about the whole situation. He can tell by that phony smile she's sporting, the incessant reassurances she's spouting, and the way she clings to him just a few seconds longer than normal when she's saying good-bye. It's small wonder then, that the child needs an emotional security blanket. That's where the wooden coathanger enters the picture.

Upon entry into Kindergarten, each child must be in possession of a wooden coathanger. To the five-year-old, the wooden coathanger is concrete proof of his existence as a functioning member of the class. Thus, when a child goes to hang up his jacket and cannot locate his wooden coathanger, the resulting extreme distress may seem out of proportion to an adult who is uninitiated in the symbolism involved. The following conversation between young children is typical:

"Where's Jamie?"

"Maybe he's sick."

"Maybe he *died!*"

"Maybe he moved to another school 'cause the teacher yelled at him yesterday."

"Let's see if his wooden coathanger is still here!"

"It's here!"

"It's OK then — he's sick today!"

Every school insists that identification be placed on every article of clothing a child may conceivably remove from his person. It really is no fun trying to divide six blue rainboots among three tearful children who look blankly at the teacher when asked their shoe sizes. I once met a Kindergarten teacher walking slowly down a hallway, twirling a small pair of panties and muttering to herself. When I gently enquired into the nature of her dilemma, she moaned, "In the letter I sent home, I explained the importance of labelling all hats, scarves, mitts, boots, and jackets. I just didn't think of *panties*."

A visitor to the Kindergarten room must be selective in timing her visit. NEVER arrive just when the kids are donning outerwear before trekking home on a cold January day. The unsuspecting visitor is invariably asked to tie a scarf by one of the more outgoing children. This gives heart to the other twenty-one, who immediately clamour for the same service to be performed for them — NOW!

Hard Cases — Kindergarten Division

Let's hope your child does not become as jaded with the Kindergarten experience as did one little girl of my acquaintance. She skipped merrily off to Kindergarten every morning for two-and-a-half weeks. One morning, her mother woke her as usual for school, only to be informed that the child had decided not to go to school that day.

"Don't you feel well?" inquired the anxious parent.

"I feel fine," responded the girl. "Sandboxes and playhouses are okay, Mum, but enough's enough!"

7

Now consider the Case of the Chronic Spitter. This little girl spat at any of her classmates who raised her ire. The patient Kindergarten teacher had talked to her about what a dirty habit spitting at someone was, had deprived her of play periods, and so forth. Nothing worked. At the end of her rope, the teacher consulted a colleague of long experience.

"Dottie, if the kid wants to spit, let her spit!" was the puzzling solution offered.

"What do you mean, let her spit?"

"Just what I say! Next time she spits at someone, get a bucket, set it in front of her and tell her that since she likes to spit, she can spit to her heart's content. She'll probably look at you as if you're crazy, smirk, and start spitting merrily into the bucket. Pretty soon the smirk will disappear, along with her saliva. That's about when she'll tell you she doesn't want to spit anymore. Insist she try a couple more spits, just to make sure she's got spitting out of her system. Then assure her that if she spits at anyone again, you'll gladly find the bucket for her. Then let her go to the water fountain to top up her fluid level and your problem should be solved!"

Dubiously, Dottie took the advice. It worked like a charm!

Say Good-bye

For half a day every weekday, for ten months, a Kindergarten teacher is in close contact with a group of five-year-olds. When the time comes for them to leave her and go to "real" school in Grade 1, that teacher has formed some pretty strong attachments.

There's Donny, chattering away twenty to the dozen to anybody who'll listen. This is the same Donny whose parents had taken baby talk to such a ridiculous degree that no one except them could understand what the boy said. The teacher knows that Donny's mother will

never quite forgive her for turning down her offer to stay in the Kindergarten classroom to act as translator.

Lisa begs to be allowed to take a note all the way to the office. At the beginning of the year she was so painfully shy that she couldn't bear to have her mother or her teacher out of her sight. For six weeks, she spoke to the teacher only when she was directly asked a question. Just that morning she was ribbing the principal about his big tummy, much to his discomfort!

What will the teacher do next year without Justin to come and give her a speechless hug every time he is on the verge of losing his temper? It had taken teacher and pupil a month of trial and error before they hit on that solution for his emotional problems.

When the time comes to write "Passed to Grade 1" on the back of the report cards, the Kindergarten teacher does so with mixed emotions. She remembers those fledglings as they were at the beginning of the year and has watched their first fluttering forays into the bigger world. She looks at the little stool she used to carry to the water fountain when they went for drinks. Now it lies discarded and scorned. The growth chart shows they've grown an average of 3 cm during the school year, and now they stretch on tiptoe, determined to be "big boys and girls".

One thing she knows: She'll miss them much longer than they'll miss her.

Starting Grade 1

Does the Teacher Have The Right Stuff?

Because Grade 1 marks the real beginning of your child's formal education, it deserves your close attention. First, and most important, you must ensure that your child gets a good Grade 1 teacher. It really doesn't matter that much who teaches your kid physics in her final year of high school. But if she doesn't have a good Grade 1 teacher, she may well a) not reach her final year of high school or b) be unable to read the word Physics. "But how am I supposed to know if the teacher who's to teach Grade 1 is good?" I hear you cry. Well, list' and ye shall learn!

In selecting a first grade teacher, you have to look for an experienced person. Here are the telltale signs of experience:

- When you meet her, she suggests, "Let's all sit down at Ms. Brown's desk."
- She talks to you in a slow and very distinct manner.
- If you move in your seat, she asks if you have to go to the washroom.
- If you decline the offer, she says, "Well, let's not squirm around. Sit up nice and straight and tall."

- If you accept the offer, upon your return she asks, "Did you wash your hands?"
- She uses no word with more than two syllables.
- When referring to numbers, she holds up the appropriate number of fingers; e.g. "We go to music three times (three digits shown) and P.E. two times (two digits raised) in a cycle."

Seek no further — you are obviously meeting a veteran!

The Big Day

The first day of school finally arrives! The eager young scholar bounds out of bed and throws on the new clothing lovingly selected by his doting mother. He bounces to the breakfast table. At this point, beware of older siblings! Right about now, big brother is apt to launch into a detailed discussion of the function of the school nurse, replete with vivid descriptions of "the little kids getting their needles." You may have to work hard to restore your young one to a semblance of his former enthusiasm.

Enrolling your child in school is an emotion-filled occasion. You just know that the woman standing at the portals of learning with the professional smile of welcome pasted on her face isn't going to love him as you do, isn't going to take the time to wiggle his loose tooth and gasp in wonderment, isn't going to realise that he's shy about asking a stranger if he may use the washroom, isn't going to understand that he sometimes puts his left shoe on his right foot. To her, he's just the same as all the others, and you know, with every fibre of your being, that this just isn't so.

As he loosens his grip on your hand, yelling, "Hey, Christopher, can I sit beside you?" the realisation will come to you that your relationship with your child has entered an entirely new phase. I think North American schools could learn from many Scottish schools, which provide an urn of tea to comfort distraught mothers who are frequently accompanied by equally distressed grandmothers and aunts. The more hard-bitten members of our profession call it Tea and Tissues Day.

THE IDEAL GRADE 1 TEACHER:

COMPLETE GLOSSARY OF 1 SYLLABLE WORDS

ALL PURPOSE HAIRSTYLE

EAGLE EYES - ABLE TO DETECT A SPITBALL AT 50 PACES

SENSITIVE NOSE - FOR SNIFFING OUT "THE CULPRIT"

TONGUE - CAPABLE OF LICKING 500 SMELLY STICKERS PER WEEK

STRONG INDEX FINGER - USEFUL FOR POINTING, SIGNALLING, REMOVING SHARP OBJECTS EARS, BOOT TYING ETC.

LARGE HEART = PATIENCE GALORE

STRONG STOMACH = LATE LUNCH BREAKS, WITH - STANDING "CLASSROOM ACCIDENTS"

ALL PURPOSE, ALL WEATHER APPAREL

NON-RUN NYLONS, STRONG KNEES SUITABLE FOR KNEELING ON GRITTY SURFACES IE CONCRETE, HALL FLOORS, LARGER STUDENTS

FLAT FEET.

16

You will probably have to fill in a form which your child will proudly proffer to you. Do it with good grace, so the teacher may avoid this typical first-day quest for basic information:

"Peter, what's your daddy's name?"

"Daddy."

"Do you know your mother's name, Peter?"

"Sure! Mummy!"

"Where does your daddy work, dear?"

"At the office."

"Does your Mummy work?"

"No. She doesn't do anything."

"Do you know your middle name, Peter?"

"Well, Mummy calls me Punkin."

"What's your phone number, Punkin?"

"Ah, it starts with a 2 and it's got a 9."

"Where do you live, Peter?"

"Right next to Christopher. He's my best friend!"

It's Love!

Realise that, somewhere in the first couple of grades, your child is going to fall in love with the teacher. Since this phenomenon has nothing to do with sex, but rather falls into the category of adoration, the gender of the principals involved is a non-issue. You will be assailed with descriptions of the teacher's smile, the teacher's clothes, the teacher's every mannerism, the teacher's wit (usually of the "Why did the chicken cross the road? To get to the other side!" calibre), the teacher's intellectual brilliance (as demonstrated by her amazing speed at counting by twos all the way to twenty) until you are quite positive that you know a great deal more about this teacher than you ever wanted to.

The first time your child calls you Ms. _____ (here substitute the name of your child's first grade teacher), take it as a compliment. After all, he must think a great deal of you if he elevates you to the same level as his teacher. If you find the experience disquieting, it's nothing to the disquiet a twenty-two-year-old newly graduated teacher feels when her sleeve is tugged and a wee voice pipes, "Mom, I can't find my pencil!"

Love of the peer group variety also occurs in the elementary grades. Many a little girl has run up to me wreathed in a beatific smile, crying, "David pushed me down in the snow and pulled off my hat and I chased him all over the playground to get it back!" This is all the evidence any red-blooded six-year-old female needs to prove she's got her man!

19

"But Ms. Brown Said ..."

Only popes and elementary school teachers have had infallibility conferred upon them. For a mere parent to cast doubts on what the teacher said is just plain foolhardy.

Asked what the air we breathe was made up of, I gave an impromptu science lesson, stating that the air was made up mostly of oxygen, with quite a bit of nitrogen and tiny little bits of carbon dioxide, argon and other stuff. After ushering my charges out at the end of the day, I began to have niggling doubts about the accuracy of the knowledge I had so confidently imparted. Upon checking, I of course discovered that the air was made up of mostly nitrogen, with only about 20 percent oxygen. Making a mental note to confess my sin the next morning, I went along home.

Next morning I was savouring a cuppa in the staff room, when one of my colleagues bore down upon me with a face like thunder. He confronted me with passing along misinformation to his son, David, who had the misfortune to be in my class that year. I readily admitted that I had reversed the quantities of oxygen and nitrogen and intended to correct my mistake that day. Since this fellow was the high school science teacher, I had to get a dig in about the illogic of all things scientific, asking him why nitrogen masks didn't drop from the ceilings of planes if the air was so chockfull of nitrogen.

21

Apparently, over the supper table, David had trotted out the garbled version of the composition of air which his father off-handedly corrected. David was adamant. Daddy, unaccustomed as he was to having his scientific pronouncements questioned, insisted that either David had misheard his teacher or his teacher was mistaken. David declared that he was sure he had quoted me accurately. Then, responded that *foolish* father, the teacher was wrong. At which point, all hell broke loose! His every entreaty, including a display of his Master's Diploma in Chemistry to his son, was met with a stony, "But Ms. Brown said!"

We both had a good laugh in the staff room. Then I dropped the bomb on him. "Just pray, Hugh, that he doesn't ask me what causes rain!"

"Why?" he asked ominously.

"Because I'll tell him two clouds bumped their heads together and started to cry!"

One family had a week of utter misery after their son had learned about the energy crisis. After his class had discussed methods of energy conservation, Larry was given a badge which conferred upon him the status of "Energy Inspector".

This little guy let the job go to his head! While watching TV, Larry's father decided to amble over to the fridge to see what he could find. As he stood contemplating the fridge's contents, Larry slammed the door and told his father that he should decide what he wanted from the fridge *before* opening the door. Otherwise, he was wasting energy! Ms. Brown said so!

Larry's mother mentioned that she was going to run a bath and have a really good soak.

23

"No, you're not! Take a shower! You'll use less hot water!" Larry barked.

After a week of this kid asking if they intended to weather strip the doors, flicking off lights and the TV if they left a room for thirty seconds, the parents were at their wits' end. They were reduced to "binging" after their son was safely asleep: they'd flick on all the lights, take forbidden baths, and hold the fridge door open just for the sheer pleasure of it.

Finally, thank heavens, Larry lost his badge! Or was it stolen?

Messages from the Front

Your kid is going to stumble home from school in the elementary grades with an awe-inspiring quantity of paper, proving her ability in math, spelling, reading, painting, drawing and printing. All, repeat ALL, of this work must be displayed prominently in your home for periods of time varying between several weeks and several months. You must understand that any failure to display ANY part of this mountain of seatwork is taken as proof positive that you don't love her. Arm yourself with a drawerful of fridge magnets and await the onslaught.

Despite the fact that your child alone has brought home enough paper to be personally responsible for the obliteration of a small forest, be prepared for the following inevitable verbal encounter:

Parent, cheerfully: "How was your day, honey?"

Child, dismissively: "Fine."

Parent, persistently: "What did you do?"

Child, positively: "Nothin'."

If you continue this game and respond "Oh come on, you must have done something!" he may allow that they went to the gym. Since

verbal communications may be scanty and unreliable, take comfort from the unending stream of paper!

Communication is, of course, a two-way street. If the messages coming home sometimes seem a little garbled — consider the hair-raising information that is being taken back to the classroom.

If you were to ask any Grade 1 teacher to explain the rationale behind having a child stand up in front of the class and tell everyone her "news," she would probably give you some spiel about the importance of developing the child's ability to verbalise her experiences, practise her listening skills, and interact with her peers in a social setting.

Horsefeathers! The real reason teachers have newstime is to cull enough information about your private life to provide them with a second source of income, should the need arise. Never breathe a word to your offspring about your mother-in-law, your estimate of the intelligence of your boss, or the state of your head on the morning following the office Christmas party. Believe me, the teacher (and all the other kids) hear them all! Herewith, a selection of actual "news-time" dillies:

"We're moving next week but I'm not supposed to tell nobody 'cause the man who owns the apartment will want all the rent money we owe him."

"My Mummy bought an ornament. She said it was a metal sculpture.

"My daddy said it was a hunk of junk and mummy should have her head examined for spending two hundred dollars on it."

"My dad was curling all weekend in the men's bonspiel. On Sunday afternoon he took a bath with all his clothes on, and he fell asleep in the tub and my mom woke him up and said he was a damn fool."

Sometimes, the teacher helps the dialogue along, unable to resist the temptation:

"Yesterday I picked up a bee and it stung me!"

"Andrew, why in the world did you pick it up?"

"I thought it was a friendly one!"

"I've got a hole in my shoe and my feet got wet walking home for lunch today."

"Did you tell your mom, Danny?"

"Yes."

"So are you getting new shoes after school today?"

"No. She told me to walk on my heels if it rains again between now and payday."

"I'm wearing the same panties I was wearing yesterday, you know."

"Really, Amanda."

"Yeah! My mom hasn't done the laundry for two weeks and I've only got fourteen pairs of panties."

"The guy my dad works beside has got his own elevator!"

"Wow! His very own elevator!"

"But it doesn't work properly, though."

"What's wrong with it?"

"My dad says it doesn't go all the way to the top floor."

Since teachers are modestly paid, if you see one driving a Caddy, you'll know the temptation to blackmail was too great to resist!

Of Sore Tummies, Sniffles, and Other Malaises

Feigning illness is not uncommon. An attack of what is commonly known as "schoolitis" will occur sooner or later. Diagnosis can be extremely difficult. You may pride yourself on your ability to spot schoolitis and you may even win a few preliminary skirmishes, but the battle always goes to the child.

At lunch, Jodie may claim to have a sore tummy, but you, clever parent that you are, note that she demonstrates no reluctance to wolf down dessert. You insist that she goes to school, stating that you're sure her sore tummy will get better. About forty-five minutes later, you are summoned to pick up your daughter from school. You will be met at the classroom door by your white-faced daughter, clinging to the hand of a greenish-looking teacher. Jodie will wail, "I threw up all over. I *told* you I had a sore tummy!"

As the reluctant scholar gains experience, he varies the approach. One fourth-grader who had pulled the tummy routine on a Tuesday morning to deflect attention from homework not done, knew that on the Wednesday morning he had to be much more inventive when he again found himself facing his teacher with her unbelieving and totally pitiless glare. Shoved out of the house by his mother, who was equally intimidated by the battle-hardened teacher, he decided to avoid direct confrontation by trying out his all-new routine on the school secretary, whom he foolishly assumed to possess a heart. With a suitably woebegone expression, he limped into the office and asked if he could go home.

"Oh! Is it your tummy again, Darren?"

"Well, no, Mrs. Prentice, it's more serious!" At this point he staggered artfully against her desk, clutched the right (or wrong!) side of his chest, declaring, "It's my heart!"

Then there's the child who is sent to school with the sniffles. How irritating it is for a teacher to be told by a parent that Carrie has a cold and should be kept indoors for recess, since the weather is so severe. Usually, the teacher cooperates. The result is that, rather than getting a set of scribblers corrected, the teacher listens to a blow-by-blow description of the entire plot of "E.T." until his eyes glaze over. When he dismisses the class for the day, the poor teacher glances out the window and watches Carrie play in the snow for half an hour in the same cold weather that prevented her from going out for a fifteen-minute recess.

The Tooth Fairy

When eight-year-old Peter lost a tooth, he regarded it as a considerable problem. As he earnestly explained to me, he knew there was no tooth fairy but he knew his mother still believed, and he was at a loss about how to break the news to her.

But my favourite tooth-fairy story concerns Kevin. One day, he lost his tooth in class. He deposited it with me for safekeeping. At the end of the day he marched off, proudly bearing the tooth in a wad of tissues.

The next morning, Kevin informed me that he had lost his tooth on the way home. Realising the magnitude of such a disaster, I started to commiserate with my charge, when I was interrupted by the somewhat cryptic statement: "It doesn't matter! All you have to do is sign this paper!" Intrigued, I unrolled the scroll of beautiful paper upon which was written, in excellent calligraphy, the words AN AFFIDAVIT TO THE TOOTH FAIRY.

In his best legalese, this lucky little chap's lawyer father had prepared a statement, with the obligatory heretofores and party of the second parts, etc., for me to sign as witness to the fact that the alleged tooth had actually existed. I happily complied and that night the AFFIDAVIT TO THE TOOTH FAIRY was left under the pillow and was replaced by the quarter from the Tooth Fairy. Funny how you can love a man you've never met!

Communication Gaps and Gaffes

Difficulties with communications pro- bably constitute the most serious prob- lem in schools today. They also are the richest source of hilarity.

Amanda's parents had given her all the usual warnings about what to do when approached by strangers. Thus, when she threw up in Grade 1, she adamantly refused to accept a ride home from the new principal, because her mother had told her never to get into a stranger's car.

Tammy, when studying Australia, had been very interested in the vast numbers of sheep and the importance of wool as a major export. Consequently, on a test, she wrote that lots of people in Australia probably earned their living by shaving sheep.

The Lord's Prayer, according to Lisa:
  Our Father, Who art in Heaven, Harold be Thy name ...

and

A rendition of *O Canada* by Robbie:
  O Canada, our home and native land
  See straight enough
  In all our sons command ...

"May I use the washroom?"

"Recess is in ten minutes, Kenny. Can you wait?"

"Okay."

A mysterious puddle appears under Kenny's desk five minutes later.

"Kenny! I thought you said you could wait!"

"I changed my mind!"

A 320 pound music teacher inspired awe (and total obedience) when he told a group of young children he would sit on anybody who was bad.

"Do you have any half scap, Mrs. Blake?"
　Totally confused, Mrs. Blake asked, "What are you doing, dear?"
　"I'm finishing writing my story and I need more paper."
　"Well, there's lots of paper right there."
　"Yes, but I'm almost finished."
　"So?"
　"Well, that's full scap and I only need a half scap."

Getting the message across to a five-year-old can be quite a challenge. There was Stephen trying to piece together a puzzle when he was joined by his helpful teacher. He explained that he couldn't get this last piece to fit into the puzzle. His teacher quickly grasped the situation and suggested that it would help if Stephen turned the piece of puzzle around. Ever cooperative, Stephen did exactly that: he clutched the piece of puzzle and turned around! When he had completed his pirouette, he regarded his teacher with a look of utter contempt and said, "That didn't help one bit!"

A puzzled mother phoned a teacher to ask where her daughter might have got the idea that the teacher was going to cut off her head. After a few moments of deliberation the teacher sheepishly explained that one of her favourite expressions was, "Heads will roll!"

One Grade 3 teacher discussed vices and virtues with his students, and then invited them to write down their greatest virtue and their greatest vice. When marking their efforts, he came across the following confession from the student who gave him the greatest headaches: "My greatest vice is that sometimes I think bad names about my teacher."

He scrawled, "And vice versa!" across the bottom of his paper. The kid nearly went crazy trying to find someone who could explain to him what "vice versa" meant!

A Grade 2 class was set the task of doing page 56 in the math textbook. After ten minutes, one very frustrated young fellow approached the teacher's desk.

"How am I supposed to do this?" he wailed. "It says 'Find the sum'. I've looked all over that page 56 and I can't find the 'sum' anywhere!"

Another young lady approached her teacher with a very perplexed look on her face.

"Are you stuck on one of the math problems, Angela?" inquired the teacher.

"Well, not really," she replied. "I'm just curious. It says here 'Farmer Jones sold his herd of 78 cattle for $80.00 a head. How much money was he paid?' I was just wondering. Don't they pay *anything* for the bodies?"

There was the teacher who explained that a diagraph was two consonants which came together to make a new sound. She then introduced the letters "s" and "h" as making the sound of 'sh'. Everyone was encouraged to make this sound. So far, so good. Then she innocently asked the class to volunteer words that contained the sound "sh".

Fish! Ship! Shop! Shape! Sheep! They came in droves! The lesson came to an abrupt halt when she informed Michael that his offering wasn't used in polite company and if reference *had* to be made to it, it was called excreta! She used quite a different teaching approach when introducing "ck"!

One teacher set her group to work on a reading comprehension test on the subject of "The Woodpecker." The children were to read the information given about the woodpecker and fill in the blanks in the sentences which followed. The teacher collected the tests at the end of the period, took her kids to music class, returned to her room and settled down to mark the test. Soon she came to a paper in which a pupil had erred rather hilariously. Instead of inserting the word "tongues" in the following sentence, the student had inserted the word "peckers": "Their _____ are long with sharp barbs on the end." A colleague later found her wandering the hallways muttering, "Talk about painful!" and laughing hysterically.

Wishing to explore the topic of our social mores, a Grade 5 teacher asked her class to think about why they obeyed their teacher. "After all," she pointed out, "there are twenty-four of you guys and only one of me. Why don't you guys rise up and say, 'OK, teach, we've had enough of you ordering us around. Now you'll have to obey us'?" She called on Scott to answer. He volunteered that the only reason he could think of was that his parents had taught him to be kind to animals! In conversation with Scott's mother a couple of days later, the teacher discovered that Scott's mother had been on the verge of infanticide until Scott had said, "Relax, Mom. Mrs. Baker laughed harder than anybody!"

A little transplanted Newfoundlander asked her teacher in Manitoba how to spell the word "vice". Upon reflection, the teacher couldn't imagine why a young child would want to use the word vice. Instead of spelling the word, she asked the child to use it in a sentence. The response was, "I have a sore t'roat and me vice is hoarse."

One young man got himself into trouble for fighting on the playground. After being chastised in the office, he returned to class and told his teacher his tale of woe. She gave him a quick hug and warned him that when he went out for recess he wasn't to let anyone get his goat.

"What goat?" the puzzled student asked.

A Grade 4 boy, who had considerable difficulty controlling his behaviour at the best of times, was having a particularly bad week. On Monday, he was given corporal punishment for hitting another student. On Tuesday, he landed in the office again for disrupting his class by pinning invitations to "Kick me!" on the backs of other students. On Wednesday, the principal met with his parents to discuss his general deportment. On Thursday, Andrew was a model of decorum, obviously induced by a little family conference. On Friday morning, Andrew continued to exhibit perfect behaviour in word and in deed.

On Friday afternoon, the class was making sock puppets, which involved sewing buttons on the sock to represent two eyes and a nose. The teacher, a liberated woman, forbade the boys to bribe the girls into doing their sewing for them. The teacher demonstrated how to sew on a button and everyone got down to the task. Now an art lesson that involved sharp needles should have tempted Andrew beyond endurance! But, no! He sat quietly, with complete concentration given to the button sewing. His face was screwed up, his tongue was stuck out of his mouth, and his entire upper torso was contorted with the effort to get the button to adhere to the sock. Suddenly, the air was rent by a loud and heartfelt, "This frigging thing!" A hush descended over the room. Andrew looked up into the eyes of his teacher and sighed, "I blew it again!"

In January, a teacher received into her room a little Japanese boy whose command of the English language was somewhat limited. She noticed that he would become confused by colloquial English. When St. Valentine's Day rolled around, it was evident that the child was not familiar with this celebration. She did her best to explain, but the whole thing remained a mystery to him. A few weeks later, the class was doing various things with a St. Patrick's Day theme, and again Hideki felt a little confused and left out, despite the teacher's efforts. On Thursday evening, Miss MacKay received a phone call from Hideki's father. The conversation went something like this:

"Miss MacKay, my son seem confused by that crock you are teaching this week."

Noting that the parent's command of colloquial English was not much better than his son's, the teacher replied, "Yes, it really is a crock, isn't it!"

"But how can I help him with this crock?" asked the concerned parent.

"Well, really, there's nothing you can do. It will all become clear to him after a few years."

"A few years!" exclaimed the father. "Do you think my son slow learner?"

"Oh, no, no!" the teacher reassured. "He is a bright little boy, but stuff like St. Valentine's Day and St. Patrick's Day are celebrations he will become familiar with the longer he stays in North America. And, anyway, as you say, they really *are* a crock. Don't worry about them."

There was quite a long silence before the father said, "No! No! I mean crock on the wall!" Miss MacKay thought furiously and could not remember teaching anything about *walls* in the past week.

"I'm sorry, Mr. Yashimoto, but I don't quite understand what you're referring to," she confessed.

"You know! The crock! Crock on the wall! Tell time!"

"Oh, *that* crock!" was the response from the teacher, as soon as she could control her voice. "I wonder if I could call you back in ten minutes?"

The Lost and Found

We live in a prosperous country. If your present circumstances tempt you to question that statement, trot along to your kid's school and ask to look in the lost and found box. The wealth of our society is revealed by the "droppings" of our children. What a treasure trove! Over the years, the sight of the riches accumulated in the 'lost and found' receptacles of various schools has inspired me to many musings.

For a start, I think Mao had the right idea. He advocated that the teeming millions should be garbed in a unisex utilitarian navy suit of clothing and the resources of the state be used instead to produce important things like tractors. If you have ever seen 1712 odd mitts being disgorged from a "lost and found", you'd be convinced he was right! Do we really need the type of economy that gives us a choice of at least 1712 different patterns for woollen mitts? If those 1712 mitts were all navy, I'll bet we could size them up and recycle them into about 856 pairs of perfectly adequate handwarmers.

The Perfect Crime

Thanks to the lost and found, I have developed the first foolproof way to commit murder. The secret lies in the discarded lunch boxes that

lie innocently in every lost and found, in every school across the country. At the beginning of each school year, every kid insists that, whether he has to eat lunch at school every day or not, he absolutely *must* have a lunch box. The parents are so skilfully conned that they come to believe that if their child doesn't get that Darth Vader/ Bugs Bunny/Miss Piggy/E.T./Mickey Mouse/Strawberry Short-cake lunchbox, the kid's academic growth will be stunted for life. Thus they shell out four or five bucks for the lunchbox, whose sole attraction is the picture of whichever character is the current darling of the pre-teen set. The child is so happy to get his lunchbox that he rushes to the kitchen whenever he gets home, pours juice in the thermos, slaps together a peanut butter sandwich and announces he's going to have a picnic in the family room. The novelty wears off quickly, though, and the lunchbox goes missing after three or four trips to school. More than likely, it is never found by its owner. It lies in the lost and found for months.

But how do you commit the perfect murder with only the lowly lunchbox as a weapon? Well, the secret lies in the fact that these lunchboxes are never empty when they are lost. Oh no! They contain maybe half a cup of chocolate milk, perhaps a half-eaten apple, a quarter of an egg salad sandwich and maybe a carton of yogurt with three spoonsful out of it. Now if such a lunchbox goes missing in action in November, by May it is a deadly weapon! The contents have fermented into a deadly brew! Now all you need is a victim. Walk the victim past the "lost and found" and casually mention the waste of money represented by the contents.

"For example," you say, "just look at that Darth Vader lunchbox. It looks brand new. I'll bet the kid didn't even check the lost and found."

Then you pick up the lunchbox and toss it to the victim with the offhand remark, "I'll bet if you opened that up, you'd find the kid's name printed right inside!"

The victim, fired up with indignation, will agree with you and fumble open the catch. That's it! One whiff and it's curtains! The death certificate will read: Death by inhalation of toxic fumes. They could never prove malice aforethought!

Scarcity and Want

Now about all that stuff that mysteriously goes missing at school. Parents get lists of necessary supplies for the upcoming school year and dutifully round up everything demanded. The credit card limit is stretched to its fullest by the time you've bought all the stuff on the supply lists and outfitted the children with jeans with knees intact and a couple of tops without stains so that the new teachers won't think your children come from a deprived home.

It is therefore understandable that you become somewhat agitated two weeks after school begins, when you start to have this type of conversation with your offspring:

"Mom, I need some pencil crayons!"

"What do you mean, you need pencil crayons?! I bought you a pack of twenty-four! Where'd they go?"

"I dunno! They're nearly all gone!"

"Mom, my erasers are gone."

"You had three of them! I'm fed up with this! You can just buy one out of your allowance!"

"But, Mom! I can't help it if my stuff gets ripped off and the teacher says I need an eraser for this afternoon and I don't get my allowance 'til Saturday!"

"Mom, I can't find one of my gym shoes at school."

"All RIGHT! I've had the biscuit! Those runners cost me twenty-two dollars and ninety-five cents! You can just get yourself to that

48

school and FIND that thing! I'm not buying any more stuff. Did you look in your locker?"

"Yeah!"

"Did you check the lost and found?"

"Yeah! The teacher told me to. But it wasn't there!"

"Are you sure you looked properly?"

"Yeah! An' it's not there!" An artful sniffle usually appears about this time.

Let's pause for clarification. Your child has stated that she has looked in the lost and found. She's not lying to you! She did look in the lost and found! She went to the box and she lifted the lid and she looked! When the gym shoe did not jump out and clutch her in an embrace and declare loudly, "Take me! I'm yours!" she concluded that it wasn't there.

Now there are two ways to deal with this situation. You can capitulate and drive her to school next morning and find the lost and found box and rummage around in it yourself. Or you can yell instructions to her about emptying and actively searching through the box with an accompanying threat such as: "You find that second runner or you won't need a second runner 'cause you'll be going to school in your bare feet!" With either approach, the chances are excellent that the missing footwear will materialize. It's all just a matter of style!

In case you're curious, what actually happens to all that leftover clothing is that it is paraded before the student body at least three times a year, to very little effect. The conversation between student and teacher goes something like this:

"Jeffrey, isn't that your gym suit? I seem to remember it was red and grey."

"No, Mrs. Baker, I've never seen that gym suit before in my life."

"Look, Jeffrey, I'm not asking you to admit ownership of a murder weapon! Just a simple gym suit! At least pick it up and look at it!"

"It's not mine!"

"How do you know?"

"It's dirty!"

"Of course it's dirty — it's been lying in that box for months! It'll wash! Those outfits are expensive! Pick it up and look at it!"

"I don't want to!" implores Jeffrey, with eyes brimming. "It's dirty!"

Faced with this reaction, lots of teachers leave it at that, consoling themselves with the thought, "Well, I tried!"

At the end of every school year, there is a massive heap of clothing and equipment which, despite teachers' entreaties, threats or bribes, no one will claim. In our school, we ship the lot to a remote community where the "unwanted" becomes the "much sought after". Packing the stuff up is a chore which the janitor regards as his most dangerous task. He can be seen on the last day of school valiantly defending his CARE package by using a whip and a chair to fend off the teachers.

Contraband

Teachers start every year with a space left empty at the back of one of their desk drawers. They are prepared! They are leaving room for the cache of contraband!

Teachers confiscate the oddest stuff. After a couple of months of school, the loot at the back of the drawers might consist of:

7 miniature race cars

1 matchbox containing Ryan's collection of dead bugs

1 vicious-looking pocketknife which Colin assures you his parents know about and approve of wholeheartedly

4 Strawberry Shortcake dolls

2 Blueberry Muffin dolls

1 Apple Dumplin' doll

1 Playboy centerfold

3 gutted pens converted to peashooters

5 collections of bubble gum hockey cards

1 slingshot constructed from rubber bands

1 brownish rock-hard orange which you forgot to return at four o'clock on the day it was confiscated

Contraband is given various terms of incarceration, depending on the nature of the contraband or the number of warnings issued by the teacher. The vicious pocketknife probably won't be returned at all, but handed to the shocked parents at the conclusion of the next parent-teacher conference. The Playboy centerfold might find its way back to the owner at week's end. It's kinda neat to smile approvingly at the owner and hand him a sealed envelope containing his centerfold and then ask him if he's ever heard of a Playboy Jigsaw Puzzle. He will very likely reply in the negative. That's when you hit him with, "Well, son, you now own a 200-piece Playboy Jigsaw Puzzle!"

It is necessary to do a general clean-out twice annually, due to the volume of contraband taken into captivity. Christmas and year-end are popular times for general amnesties, no doubt due to the general goodwill fostered by both seasons.

Attention-Getting Devices

Students use a variety of methods to attract a teacher's attention.

Young children use the cry, "Teacher!" quite indiscriminately. Any person over five feet in height is designated "Teacher." It makes not the slightest difference to a six-year-old if the person is a teacher, a teacher's aide, a janitor, a principal, or the person who's here to fix the heating. If the little one gets some action, who cares what you call the big one?

Young children have the disconcerting habit of tugging at the clothing of the teacher. They can stop you dead in mid-stride, so this is really a very effective attention-getting tactic. The attention-getting device that really amuses me is the Kindergarten Klutch. You're standing there and some little guy comes up and grabs some part of your anatomy and cries, "Teacher!" You ask him what he wants as you are disengaging his paw from wherever he's planted it. You really can't help but reflect that if he were fifteen years older, modesty would demand that you slap his face!

In every class you'll find the finger-snapper. Every hand is up and everyone is desperate to answer the question posed by the teacher! One student figures that snapping his fingers will give him that extra edge over the competition. Wrong! I find that the best way to eliminate this irritating practice is to bark loudly while approaching the student on all fours! Everybody gets the message!

Some students favour going into transports of ecstasy. They stand out from the crowd anxious to answer a question by jumping out of their seats and doing a little dance before subsiding into their seats again and repeating the procedure at five-second intervals. Or else they throw their arms out in a passable imitation of the Nazi salute and grunt, "Uh! Uh!" loudly and passionately. Or they may pump their arms up and down to the point of risking dislocation while they chant, "Oh! Me, please, Mrs. Baker! I know! Oh! Me, please, Mrs. Baker! I know!" incessantly. Choosing someone to answer can be a truly harrowing experience for a teacher!

Smart Kids

Very intelligent kids scare me. They catch on too easily; they question my pronouncements when I am trying to come across as the modern day equivalent of the Oracle of Delphi.

Fortunately, children of average intelligence are completely unawed by their friends who are endowed with more of the grey matter. Communication goes on, but occasionally someone fumbles the conversational ball.

Jared, a highly cerebral eight-year-old, was eating lunch with a classmate at school one day. For some minutes he studied Mary's hairdo, which was highlighted by an extremely short ponytail that started very high on her head and stuck straight up in the air. Gnawing on a chicken leg, Jared casually remarked, "Mary, your ponytail makes you look like you've been electrocuted."

"Oh, thank you, Jared!" Mary delightedly responded. Jared looked a little disconcerted for a few seconds, shrugged, and took another bite of chicken.

I once overheard a group of nine-year-olds discussing ghosts. They were arguing back and forth about whether ghosts really exist,

citing movies they had seen, stories their grandmothers had told them, and so on. After five minutes of rather inconclusive discussion, Barbie brought the matter to an end by authoritatively stating, "Look, you guys, you've got to realise that a ghost is just the spiritual manifestation of a physical entity."

As an introduction to a story about Leonardo Da Vinci, I asked a Grade 6 class to tell me anything they knew about him. I waited expectantly for someone to mention the Mona Lisa or one of Leonardo's many inventions. At last Cathy volunteered, "I understand he was homosexual."

"That's quite possibly true, Cathy," I stuttered. "But don't you know anything about the famous paintings he produced or his inventions?" I asked, in an effort to get this lesson back on track. Before Cathy could respond, what I feared actually happened:

"What's a homosexual?" came a chorus of voices.

"Well, probably the teacher can explain that better than I can," declared Cathy.

When you teach in a school where just the mention of sex education produces apoplexy in a vocal minority of parents, how do you respond? I took a deep breath, swore to myself I'd sue if they fired me, and launched into an explanation geared to their level. Eventually, we got around to discussing Leonardo. Interestingly, the students were a lot more interested in Leonardo's helicopter than they were in Leonardo's homosexuality.

Upon being told we were going to do art one afternoon, Jason begged to be allowed to do something else, claiming that he hated art because he couldn't draw. Remembering my own agonies over art periods in my schooldays, I agreed that Jason could do anything he pleased, as long as it was worthwhile. At the end of the period, I asked Jason to show me what he had done.

"Well," said he, "I'm very interested in the human eye, so I thought I'd find out about it in the encyclopedia. I've made a picture to show how it works. Would you like to see?"

This seven-year-old, who hated art because he couldn't draw, showed me a beautifully proportioned, technically correct drawing of an eye.

Surprises, Shocks, and Harrowing Experiences

Many teachers start their first jobs woefully lacking in the knowledge that really matters. They have studied the educational principles laid down by Rousseau and espoused the democratic principles of John Dewey. But there are many shocks and surprises in store for them. In later years, of course, the harrowing experiences still occur, but it takes more — much more — to faze the experienced teacher. The very first day of teaching is a shocker! The novice has prepared a pile of work for the class. He or she hands out the first set of seatwork, carefully explains the instructions, and tells them to go to it. That's when somebody asks if he may sharpen his pencil. The teacher says that of course he may. Another asks the same question and the teacher — fatal error! — says that anyone who needs to use the sharpener may do so. Pandemonium! Total chaos! Suddenly twenty-six kids are pushing and shoving to use the one sharpener in the room. In four years of training, not one lecturer had prepared the hapless teacher for this particular reality!

Who expected to have to be proficient at unzipping flies? There's the new teacher, supervising the Grade 2 class on washroom break. Dwayne comes out of the boys' washroom and approaches in a half-crouch.

"My zipper's stuck! Can you pull it down for me?" he asks. So the teacher crouches down and tries to yank the zipper free, but it's not budging. Then Dwayne starts dancing up and down and says, "Hurry up! I really gotta go!"

The teacher tells him to stand still. And he does stand still for three-and-a-half seconds, but the inexperienced teacher still can't move it. Desperate, she summons a colleague with a few years of primary teaching behind her. The veteran expertly frees the zipper and turns to the newcomer with a sardonic smile. "You'd better get some practice in, kid, if you're going to survive in this business!" she says.

One teacher, all unsuspecting of what lay in wait, was teaching the difference between concrete and abstract nouns. He explained that a concrete noun was something that you could see or touch or smell or taste or hear, such as desk, bacon, noise, and so forth. An abstract noun was basically an idea that existed in your mind. He asked the class if they had ever seen hatred. No, they agreed, they hadn't, although they recognized it was something that existed. He then asked if the class had ever seen happiness. Again, they agreed that it existed, although they had never seen it. Heartened, the teacher asserted that love was an abstract noun because it existed, although you could not see love. Disaster! A chorus of voices disagreed!

"I've seen love, Mr. Jackson!"

"I've seen love! Was my dad ever mad!"

"I've seen love! My mom said you should always knock! Now I remember to knock!"

"*Fairness!*" yelled the teacher. "Has anybody actually seen *fairness?*"

Creativity is a biggie in educational circles. When a colleague came to chat, a primary teacher told her students to "be snakes." Very creative! When they were satisfactorily squirming on the floor, the teacher stepped out of the room and visited with her colleague. She was a little annoyed when, after a minute, Joe interrupted to ask, "What do snakes eat?"

"I don't know!" she snapped. "Why are you even asking such a question, Joey?"

"Larry's eating flies!" came the reply.

One fourth grade teacher was really pleased with the reading lesson she had conducted in which the class had discussed the cultural differences which exist in any nation. As an example of cultural differences, she cited the fact that a dinner guest in an Arabian country was expected to burp loudly at the table to express his appreciation of the meal he had been served. She noted that if we behaved that way in our culture we would produce quite a different reaction.

Ever curious, her pupils decided to experiment! In the reading circle the next morning they reported their findings. Dennis was

64

sent to his room. Peter's father gave him a cuff on the ear. Lori's mother told her she wasn't in Arabia. How to make yourself popular in one easy lesson!

A teacher one morning instructed his students to bring a variety of materials, such as string, wool, thread, etc., for their art class that afternoon, as they were going to make a collage. Everyone turned up with an array of materials and the art lesson was a great success. Half an hour after dismissal of his class, the teacher received a call from a distraught parent who asked if the teacher had any idea why her son had a great chunk missing from the new sweater his grandmother had sent him.

Sometimes teachers turn the tables by delivering a surprise or two to their pupils. There was, for example, the teacher who told her Grade 1 kids to tidy up their desks. To encourage them to make a good job she informed them that the Jolly Green Giant would be coming in to inspect the desks while they slept. A few brave souls dared to express skepticism.

The temptation was too great! Imagine the bug-eyed faces and awed silence when those kids walked in the next morning and beheld fifteen giant green felt footprints!

All kids adore being frightened. Grimm was well-named! Little children beg to hear a scary story and plead to have the lights turned out to create the right atmosphere. Delicious little shivers of anticipation run up and down their spines. If they are seated in a semicircle around the teacher's chair, it's a riot to watch them quietly inch closer to that chair as the story unfolds until, as the climax approaches, they can get no closer. At this point it is not uncommon for them to clutch frantically at the teacher's limbs. At the completion of the tale, they exhale great sighs of relief and satisfaction and accuse each other of being scared. Then they beg for more!

Finding out the teacher's first name is considered quite a coup. Four little fellows were huddled together one afternoon. As I passed the group, I overheard Mark whisper to his buddies, "I saw a letter addressed to her sitting on her desk. Honest to God, her name is Alien!"

"I *knew* there was something queer about her!" said Tony, in awed tones.

When I reached the staff room I informed their teacher that she probably wouldn't have any discipline problems for the rest of the year.

"What do you mean?" asked Aileen.

The "Four Eyes" Syndrome

If the eye doctor tells you your kid has to wear glasses, take it as proof that you have angered the gods. Nothing brings greater grief than a young child placed in charge of a pair of eyeglasses.

A parent's first reaction, on being informed that her child needs glasses, is guilt. "I've passed on defective genes to my baby!" agonizes the bespectacled mother. "Why was I so irresponsible as to marry a man with defective genes?" says the wife of the bespectacled father. "How come he needs glasses?" the 20-20 father asks suspiciously of the 20-20 mother.

Because of guilt, parents commit the classic error. They reason that if their poor baby is unfortunate enough to require glasses because of some shortcoming in the gene pool, the best they can do is let him choose the frame he likes best. Oh dear! Given the opportunity, every child opts for wire frames at 130 bucks. Parents eye the 49 dollar el cheapos longingly, but say nothing. They might venture, "Dear, how about these frames here? They look sturdier."

The inevitable response is, "They're ugly! I hate them! I don't want to wear dumb glasses anyway! All the kids are going to call me Four-eyes".

"Well, if these are the frames you *really* like, we'll get them, dear."

This is where the teacher (me) comes in. Sean marches into class with glass case in one hand and note for me in the other. The note asks if I will ensure that Sean wears his glasses in school. At this point, I note the frames, lavishly admire the new glasses and remark how great Sean looks wearing them — and say to myself, "Stage One."

Stage Two happens along in about two weeks. Sean comes in after recess and dangles a pair of mangled spectacles before me, remarking casually, "I broke my glasses."

Stage Three comes when Sean walks in with a new pair of glasses, which may or may not be wire framed, and a note for me. The note asks if I can remind Sean not to wear his glasses out at recess.

Stage Four is reached anywhere from four days to four weeks later. I might hear a hideous yelp in the room and turn to discover that Amanda has stepped on Sean's glasses, which he had left on the floor when he was doing art. Amanda is crying and protesting, "I'm sorry! It was an accident! I'm sorry! It was an accident!" Sean is looking definitely concerned and intoning, "My parents will kill me!"

Stage Five occurs when Sean comes in with a new pair of glasses, which are definitely *not* wire frame, and a note for me. The note asks if I will ensure that Sean wears his glasses at all times with the exception of recess.

Stage Six comes when Rob knocks Sean's glasses off with a basketball in the gym and Kevin runs over them with a scooter. Rob and Kevin do a duet of, "I'm sorry! It was an accident! I'm sorry! It was an accident!" Sean slowly shakes his head back and forth, his eyes fill with tears, and he wails, "My parents will kill me for sure!"

Stage Seven rolls along. This is when Sean comes in wearing the 49 dollar el cheapos with an elastic strap around his head and a note for me. The note asks if I can ensure that Sean keeps the elastic strap on his glasses at all times, although he doesn't like it.

Stage Eight is heralded in by the tinkle of one of Sean's lenses falling on his desktop. He snatches it up and runs to me crying, "Can you put it in, Mrs. Baker? It just fell out! Can you fix it?"

"Well, Sean, maybe I can get it back in, but it will be loose and you might lose the lens. I don't want to use glue or tape, so you'd better tell your mother about it when you get home."

"But she'll freak out!"

"Now, don't worry! I'll be your witness! It wasn't your fault! You can have your mother phone me if she likes!"

Stage Nine has arrived when I behold Sean trotting in with the wandering lens held firmly in place by strips of tape along the edges. He hands me a note which asks me to excuse the state of Sean's glasses but he has an appointment next week with the optician.

Stage Ten. Ah! Stage Ten! I can relax at last! Stage Ten is when the new glasses come and the inevitable happens. But Sean copes! If the lens falls out, he borrows my tape and does a pretty creditable repair job. If they're stepped on and broken in two at the bridge he picks them up, dusts them off and uses half a roll of tape to render them serviceable once again. As the rest of the year progresses, the kid develops all the proficiency of an optical repair technician.

The only chancy part about children and eyeglasses is ensuring that the parents retain both sanity and financial solvency long enough to reach Stage Ten.

I was chatting with a new colleague who was explaining that she didn't really want to return to work that year because she thought her children were still too young for both parents to be working. I asked why she hadn't stayed home one more year. "Well, both our boys wear bifocals," she explained simply.

The Parent-Teacher Interview

Let's face it, it can be intimidating! To properly prepare for the dreaded occasion, you must decide if you want to be told what you *need to know* or what you *want to hear*. A surprisingly large number of teachers are willing to accommodate you in this regard. Ever the optimist, I'm going to assume you belong to the "need to know" group.

Beware of educationese! What possible use is it to average parents to be told that their offspring is functioning at the third level on the scale of taxonomy as determined by evaluation which has encompassed the diagnostic, formative and summative areas, which indicates that his strengths lie in the affective rather than the cognitive domain? When confronted by this type of response, the best tactic is to state, *authoritatively*, that you have recently read a simply *fascinating* piece of research which strongly indicates that there appears to be a definite inverse correlation between use of obscurantism and teacher competence.

When today's buzz words are "unmotivated" and "hyperactive", it takes a person of uncommon courage to suggest that maybe your kid is lazy or a little terror.

Give each criticism the merit it deserves. If the worst thing the teacher has to say is that Jessica doesn't colour neatly, don't lose any sleep over it. If you're told Jonathan can't clearly enunciate the "s" sound at the stage of his growth when you figure the song "All I Want For Christmas Is My Two Front Teeth" was written especially for him, don't ask for a referral to a speech pathologist.

It is hugely amusing to tell a parent that his child has an unfortunate tendency to use profane language in class when you know that the odds are pretty good the shocked response will run something like, "Holy *!G#! He swears in class? I'll be damned if I know where the little ©£*!! picks it up!"

At a parent-teacher interview, I was once complimented on the effectiveness of my lessons on mammals. When I asked the parent why she considered my lessons had been effective, she told me the following tale. Her son, Gordy, had been playing outside in his swimming trunks with the little girl next door. Gordy's mother was working at the kitchen sink and could hear the children's chatter streaming through the open window.

Neighbour girl: "Ha! Ha! You've only got one piece to your bathing suit, Gordy, and I've got two."

Gordy: "That's because you need two pieces. I only need one."

Neighbour girl: "Why do I need two pieces?"

Gordy: "You have to cover your gonads!"

A parent-teacher-specialist conference was called one afternoon to discuss speech therapy being recommended for a little girl in Kindergarten. The parents turned up and the speech therapist did her spiel about Jennifer's pronounced lisp and the need to start her on therapy as soon as possible. The parents drank in the information and when the teacher asked if they consented to treatment, the father replied, "Yeth! Thertainly!"

It should be noted that personality conflicts can and do arise between teacher and student. Sometimes, the wisest course is to have the child placed in another classroom at the same grade level. Just a word of caution, though. If your child has a "personality conflict" with just about every teacher he has, maybe, just maybe, you should take a close look at your kid. If the Grade 1 teacher tells you he doesn't apply himself, you may take comfort in the thought that she just doesn't understand your Matthew. If Matthew's second grade teacher dares to imply he's lazy, you may conclude she's awfully demanding on kids of his tender years. If, in Grade 3, you're told Matthew is capable of much better work, you may confront him with the accusation and be completely convinced that the charges are nonsense when Matthew weeps piteously on your shoulder.

The personality conflict bit can go on for as long as you want it to last. I swear I have sat across from a woman who sincerely stated that in the twelve years her son had attended school, he had encountered only one "good" teacher who understood him and didn't tell her that her boy was lazy. When she named this paragon of virtue who understood her son, everything fell into place for me. That guy was as lazy as her kid!

Highlights of the School Year

You won't hear much about the humdrum of school life from your kids, but you'll sure get filled in about the "fun stuff."

Class Party

A class party can occur anywhere from once to seventeen times a year, depending upon the gullibility of the teacher. As well as a Christmas party and a Hallowe'en party, students are liable to suggest a Thanksgiving party, A Remembrance Day party, a summer solstice party, Brad's dog's birthday party, and so on.

The class party is a dream to organize. All the teacher has to do is remind everyone to bring a snack and tapes. Everyone troops in at one o'clock, listens to the afternoon announcements over the intercom, and then asks if snacks can be eaten now. Upon being told it's only five after one, they insist that they are *starving*. The teacher mutters ineffectually that there's to be no complaining about having nothing to eat after recess, and the great eat-in commences. Each snack consists of half a loaf of peanut butter and jelly sandwiches, two pieces of fruit, a bag of chips, a chocolate bar, a can of pop and twenty-seven chocolate chip cookies (kindly supplied by well-meaning mothers). The tapes blare out "Pops for Tots" and the kids

yak with their mouths full of their own and everyone else's snacks. The teacher, sincerely wanting the kids to have a good time, may suggest that everyone start dancing or playing party games. This effort is met with pitying stares. Obviously the teacher knows nothing about having a good time. At the end of the time allotted for the festivities, the kids launch into the clean-up and declare that they sure had a *great* party.

Field Trip

The field trip is an unforgettable experience, especially for the parent who is a first-time "volunteer helper." Kids visit the fire hall, museums, zoos, legislatures, the post office, a hospital, a police station, and so on throughout their school years. Teachers like to have an adult-student ratio of about one to six. Thus the need for volunteers. If you volunteer, and turn up to find that your kid has been placed in the teacher's group — start worrying! The group in the teacher's charge is always made up of known offenders! They're the ones who will have a crack at sliding down the pole at the fire hall without waiting to be invited. They're the ones who will let a monkey get its paw tangled in their hair and then stand bellowing so that they can be heard all over the zoo. They're the ones who will try to undo a cop's holster to try out the gun.

Occasionally, because of the composition of a class, it is impossible for the teacher to accommodate all of the hellions in her own group. When this happens, she tries to choose the most aggressive parent to cope with the overflow. This can backfire! This can definitely backfire! Once, having chosen my six worst habitual criminals, I had to dispose of one live-wire, Paul, to one of my three parent volunteers. I chose Mrs. Paterson, because she had done a tour of duty with me before, knew the drill, and wasn't afraid to bark out an order now and

again. Off we went to the egg hatchery. We had a lovely time looking at the hens, watching the chicks being "sexed," seeing eggs being "candled." We were just preparing to leave, when I spied "The Look" in Paul's eyes. Mrs. Paterson had him standing right beside her, but the poor woman couldn't be expected to recognize "The Look." This ability came only after long experience in dealing with Paul. "He's all the way across the room!" I agonized to myself. "How can I get to him on time? What is it he's thinking of doing? Look around, you fool, find the temptations!" My eyes hit on the bucket full of eggs a fraction of a second before Paul's foot unobtrusively tipped it over.

Pet Day

Pet Day requires a lot of preparation. Teachers have to get the ground rules clearly laid out. It's not enough to say that the pet must be small. Mice are small. Snakes can be small. It's not enough to say that the pet must be harmless. Garter snakes are harmless. White mice are harmless. If the teacher doesn't like snakes or mice, it's much better to establish the ground rules with something like, "If anybody brings a snake or a mouse into this classroom on Pet Day, I'll pickle them. And I ain't talking about the snakes or mice." Tasteful, yet effective.

One teacher of my acquaintance was caught unawares. A sweet little girl offered to bring in a monstrous wasps' nest left over after the exterminators had finished in her home. The teacher eagerly accepted. He received the nest and placed it in a corner of the science lab until he could get around to teaching the appropriate lesson on insects.

The hitch came when he tried to enter his lab on Monday morning. Over the weekend, the heat of the lab had persuaded the wasps that

had survived the exterminator's onslaught to venture out. The result was that the guy opened his lab Monday morning to find the entire room taken over by wasps who, with all the fervour of the born-again, tried to exterminate him in two minutes or less.

The students were treated to the sight of their teacher going forth to do battle, armed with a large net covering his head and a long pipe filled with pungent Dutch tobacco. He won! But only just!

Gifts for Parents

Children sometimes candidly admit that schools are essential. After all, where else would they get the chance to produce, at no cost to themselves, cards and gifts for every social occasion? What parent hasn't been the recipient of a pencil holder constructed from a tin can and popsicle sticks? What mother hasn't swallowed an awfully big lump in her throat when she reads the handmade, misspelled Mother's Day card that arrives on the breakfast tray with the cold toast and underdone boiled egg?

A mother might spend months agonizing over the right *look* for her living room, haggling over the purchase of the just-so fabric and the perfect chesterfield, and ransacking five shopping malls to find the one lamp that will *work* in the decor she is so painstakingly constructing. To place a vase made from a toilet roll filled with carnations constructed from pink Kleenex tissues amid this splendour is surely the most tangible proof of a mother's love!

... And Gifts for Teachers

Why do little kids and/or their parents assume that female teachers still use lace hankies? It's amazing how many lace hankies teachers

have lying at the back of their dresser drawers. Personally, I haven't used a lace hankie since my mother quit doing my washing and ironing!

Why is it that only male elementary teachers ever get booze for a gift? As women rake in the hankies they'll never blow into and chocolates that head straight for their hips, their male colleagues get enough loot to stock a moderate-sized bar. Do parents honestly believe the schoolmarms of today don't let demon rum pass their lips? Surely not!

You know the lady who goes "ding-dong" at your door? I figure that woman represents a corporation that should singlehandedly fund teacher pensions. After all, those people make a fortune on teachers! Every Christmas and year-end, we are inundated with their products. I think the packaging appeals to little minds: What child can resist a bottle of perfume that, when emptied, can double as a salt shaker? Or a bottle of aftershave lotion that can do duty as an antique car ornament?

I sound as if I have been totally unappreciative of all the gifts that children have given me over the years. Not so! Each one says "I like you" or "I love you" or "Thank you for helping me". I truly am touched by the sentiments expressed by the gifts, and sincerely thank each donor. The fact that I don't care for strident perfume in no way diminishes the thought behind the gift. As a matter of fact, I have a collection of cards that accompanied gifts given to me over the years. These I treasure. A card given to me at year-end that says, "Your a grate teacher" could be used to prove my incompetence in the teaching of English, but I prefer to go with the sentiments of the writer.

Unsung Heroes, School Division

Janitors

Janitors are a unique group. They spend school breaks washing, stripping, and waxing floors, and on the first day of school they are *shattered* when the thundering herd obliterates their efforts in two minutes flat. You'd think they'd learn! School janitors either detest kids or they love them; there's no in-between. They either lurk in hallways and washrooms to get evidence of wrongdoing to present gleefully to the principal, or they can be seen listening attentively to a ten-year-old's vague description of the type of back board he needs for his Science Fair project.

Occasionally, a janitor is called upon to go on safari, in search of various small rodents that have escaped from cages in primary classrooms. When, after crawling through the entire ventilation system of the school, the janitor triumphantly enters the Grade 2 room bearing their pet guinea pig, he knows what it is to be a *hero*! A strong stomach and the ability to smile reassuringly are essential when the janitor is called upon to clean up the evidence of Susan's upset stomach.

A peculiar thing happens to a lot of janitors. The longer they are caretakers in a school, the more likely they are to suffer from the delusion that they actually are in charge of the school. Thus, the principal is constantly assailed with casual comments like:

"Terrific noise coming from that new teacher's room. Sure hope her discipline's okay."

"There's Mr. Kemp just walking in now. That's twice this week he's been late."

"Well, I've finished cleaning up the latest mess in Mrs. Love's room. They were making relief maps or something out of paper mâché. Seems to me she should teach more and make less."

A good janitor is worth his weight in gold. Many teachers consider it is more important to get along with the janitor than it is to get along with the principal. It's not the principal who conjures up an extra filing cabinet for you at the beginning of the year or finds an extra big desk for the tallest student in your class.

The janitor is probably the first adult a little first grader sees when he comes into school ten minutes late. Being ten minutes late is no big deal to you or me. But it is when you're six years old. A good janitor knows this. He'll bend down and wipe away the tears and hold that tiny hand inside his reassuring big fist as he walks the latecomer to the classroom. He'll even do the talking when the kid gets to the room and the kid is sure that's why the teacher smiles at her and says she can sit down. She can tell that janitor isn't even a teensy bit scared of the teacher!

A good janitor is the type of guy who doesn't yell at a little boy when he uses the girls' washroom by mistake. He understands that some fellas just haven't caught on to that reading stuff just yet.

Class Visitors

Occasionally, intrepid or naive visitors agree to come to the school to discuss their jobs with students. Children are dangerously unpredictable. The only question my students could think of to ask our town's mayor was, "How much money do you make?"

A six-foot-three Mountie was left alone with a Grade 1 group for a few moments and when the teacher returned the man was on the verge of complete panic. Someone was spitting on his regulation-issue boots and buffing them with the chalkboard eraser, to see if spit and polish really did get his boots that shiny. Somebody else was attacking his holster for a closer examination of his revolver. A little girl was prancing around the room wearing his hat. Two boys were busily undoing his tunic buttons to see what he was wearing underneath. After his rescue he was heard to exclaim, "Gimme those bad dudes anytime. At least you know what to expect!"

After a tour of the hospital, a Grade 2 class invited a local doctor to come to speak to them. The obliging physician turned up and patiently explained the various examinations a child might undergo. He produced his stethoscope and explained its function. He invited a little fellow in the front row to try it out. After listening intently for a few minutes, the little guy asked, "How come it doesn't play music?"

The School Photographer

The visit of the school photographer causes a transformation in any class of kids. On the morning they are having their pictures taken, they arrive looking as if they're all in competition for the title of Most Beautiful Child. Their skin is glowing. Their clothing is bright and pressed. Their hair is immaculately coiffed. Everyone has been ordered to stay clean, smile brightly, and keep their hair unmussed. An hour later, when we're called to have our pictures snapped, a metamorphosis has taken place. Not one vest has a button buttoned, not one bow on the frilly blouses remains tied, not one clip-on tie is

clipped on at both ends, Tim has managed to get green felt pen on his front teeth, and Sandi is crying because she has glue on her sleeve.

The teacher turns into a whirling dervish. Vests get buttoned, bows get tied, ties get clipped, Tim's teeth are scrubbed with a balled-up Kleenex and Sandi is assured that if she poses with her arms folded no one will ever see the glue. The teacher's personal comb is produced and everybody gets a fast "comb-out," while the teacher prays, silently and fervently, that nobody has "cooties" in their hair.

Your actual school photographer is a breed apart. If a guy can produce smiles on the faces of upwards of six hundred kids per day, day in, day out, he cannot remain unscarred for long. He stands behind a camera and keeps up a non-stop stream of sure-fire gut-splitters, while a teacher positions kids on a chair and yanks them off at a rate of ten students per minute. The repartee goes something like this:

"Hi sweetie! Bet you make the other girls jealous!"

"Hello, big fella! Married yet?"

"Front teeth missing! Tooth fairy good to ya?"

"Look at your teacher! She's mean, isn't she?"

"Hockey sweater! Going in the NHL?"

"Who's your boyfriend, honey?"

"Think Grandma will like that pretty top?"

"Bet you've got about ten girlfriends, eh, fella?"

The kids are completely enraptured. After the two minutes and thirty seconds it takes to process the average class, the kids spend ten minutes swapping the witticisms the photographer has bestowed on each of them.

Having coffee with one of those guys is really disconcerting, though. The machine-gun delivery carries over into normal conversation:

"Hello, Mrs. Baker! Having a well-earned rest, eh? Have a good summer? Me, too. See ring? Million dollar club! Yep! Figure I've taken two point five million school pictures. Been with National fifteen years. Won a trip! Yep! Quebec City! Wife loved it! Great city! Walls! History! Marvellous!"

Right about then, I'd "remember" I had hall duty!

"Subs"

A word must be said here about substitute teachers. My admiration for this group of people is unbounded. They march into classrooms all over our country every morning and take the worst abuse imaginable. Personally, I'd sling hash before I tried to earn my keep as a sub.

When I was on maternity leave from school, I was visited by the principal one Friday evening. He enquired solicitously after my health, complimented me on how well I looked, and casually asked if I had a babysitter set up. I explained that a friend was willing to babysit for me when I returned to school in two more weeks. He pussyfooted around some more, until my suspicions were well and truly aroused. Ordered to get to the point, he confessed that, that afternoon, he had lost the second sub out of my room. Like her predecessor, she had exited in tears, vowing never to return. After spending an hour on the phone, the principal was convinced that the word had got around and he would never secure a sub for my class come Monday morning. Like any teacher worth her salt, I took umbrage at the suggestion that *my kids* were bad. I assured the principal I'd be in come Monday morning and the saints preserve anyone who said a word against my class.

On Monday morning I had to endure a lot of ribbing in the staff room about the principal having to bring in the heavy artillery. Somebody asked if I had my whip with me for my role as lion tamer. My coming had been noised abroad before the nine o'clock bell so that I entered my room to find everyone seated in perfect order with shy little smiles playing around their mouths. We looked at each other for some moments before I broke the ice.

"What's this I hear about you guys being bad?"

They explained everything! Those subs didn't correct the spelling the way I did. When the second sub showed them how to do long division, even Charles, the smartest kid in the whole class, didn't understand one bit. Those subs never smiled! It was just as I had suspected — Those teachers just didn't understand my kids!

School Secretary

To be able to cope as a secretary in a school, you need to be able to do a lot more than answer the phone, type a letter, and run an office. Experience as an emergency room nurse would be beneficial, because you will often be called upon to make a snap decision on the necessary treatment for the many wounds presented to you. If you've spent a couple of years at the U.N., you'll have the diplomatic background to cope with irate parents who are convinced the principal is out to get their kids, irate teachers who are convinced the principal is out to get them, and paranoid principals who are convinced everyone is out to get principals. If you've ever been on the Grand Prix circuit, this will serve you well when you're called upon to drive hell bent for leather to the hospital with a kid whose thumb is hanging off his hand after an encounter with a power saw in Industrial Arts.

Where the Buck Stops

There are no particular qualifications needed to be a school administrator, although traditionally, it has helped to be male. To define what the administration actually does in a school is rather difficult. One newly appointed administrator, aware of the pack-rat tendencies of Grade 1 teachers, was en route to the Grade 1 classroom with a load of cardboard which she knew they would find 101 uses for. She was met by a colleague who stopped in his tracks and said, "You're delivering cardboard! So *that's* what administrators do!"

"Essentially, yes! But to be a good administrator, you must deliver cardboard with panache!" came the reply. Really, that about sums it up.

If you want my pet peeve against administrators, it's those guys who walk into your class on payday and turn super *cute*.

They wave the envelope in the air and say, "Now, everyone, this is payday for the teachers! Do you think I should pay Mrs. Baker?"

He waits for the inevitable and unanimous chorus of *"No!"* Then he continues, "Has she been good to you this month?"

Again, "NO!"

"Has she been an old meanie?"

"YES!"

"Well, I'll pay her this month," he concedes. "But she'd better smarten up next month! Will you tell me if she is mean to you next month?"

"YES!"

Then he hands over the envelope, pleased as Punch at his own rapier wit. The next month he goes through exactly the same routine and exits no less pleased with himself. Actually, it's the kids who bring the thing to a close, because they get tired of chanting "Yes!" or "No!" at the appropriate times. The poor principal is always so disappointed! Personally, I'd be willing to forego a month's pay just for the pleasure of stuffing that cheque up his nose!

I'll never forget the look on my first principal's face when he walked into my classroom and was met by what must have looked like, by his standards, total confusion.

Everyone was busy doing something "arty" and I was nowhere to be found. This man's teaching background was high school Latin. Some twit had decided this was excellent experience for an elementary school principal and — voila! — here he was surveying a third grade room where not one child was at his or her desk. He was quite convinced that learning did not take place in such an atmosphere.

"Where's your teacher, boys and girls?" he asked weakly.

"She's under the table!" came the chorus.

"May I ask *why* she's under the table?"

102

"She's making another batch of paper mâché," one of the children explained.

At this point I emerged, covered with goo to the elbows, and gave him my most dazzling smile. Perfectly aware of his conservative philosophy, I invited him to survey the activity in progress. Then I leaned toward him and whispered, "The question you must ask yourself is not, 'But is it art?' It must instead be, 'But is it education?'"

I confess to having spent some time as an administrator. But I was a failure! You see, I couldn't keep my face straight!

Picture me sitting behind my desk. The door is thrown open. Enter the elementary phys. ed. teacher. She's mad! Lordy, is she mad! Right now I have to make an important distinction. There are teachers who angrily burst into an administrator's office, maybe three times a day. After awhile, you ignore them. When a topnotch teacher bursts into your office and tells you she's mad and you know this is the first time in six months she's done it, then you listen! I invited her to have a seat and tell me the problem.

"Okay! I've got Jamie's* Grade 2 and they're getting changed after the gym class. I hear a bunch of squealing coming from the change room, so I walk in there and there's Jamie shooting everybody with a water pistol!"

"Oh! Is that all?" I interjected.

"Wait — you haven't heard it yet! The reason they're all yelling so hard is that Jamie has peed in the water pistol and he's spraying them with it!"

---

*I should explain that classes are normally known by the teacher's name, such as Mrs. Bechman's Grade 2. Sometimes, though, they are known by the principal troublemaker, such as Jamie's Grade 2.

104

What would your reaction be? Personally, I fell out of my chair laughing! The phys. ed. teacher did not share my mirth. She told me in no uncertain terms that she had Jamie waiting outside and she was going to bring him in and I had better put the fear of God into this kid. I solemnly swore I would deal with Jamie if she just gave me a moment to compose myself. Feeling I was sufficiently calm, I told the phys. ed. teacher to march in the offender.

"Well, Mrs. Miner, what can I do for you?"

"I'm having a problem with Jamie, Mrs. Baker, and I'd like you to hear about it."

"So, Jamie, we're having a problem! Would you like to tell me what the problem is?"

"Well, Mrs. Baker, I sprayed everyone with my water pistol in the change room."

"And what was in this water pistol, Jamie?"

"Wee-wee, Mrs. Baker."

"Whose wee-wee, Jamie?"

"My wee-wee, Mrs. Baker."

"Jamie? Do you mean to tell me you wee-weed into your water pistol and sprayed your wee-wee all over the boys in your class?"

"Yes, Mrs. Baker," he replied, shamefaced.

"Jamie, that is disgusting! You should be ashamed of yorself!"

"I am, Mrs. Baker!"

"Jamie, in all the world, what made you do such a thing?"

"Well ... I really had to go!" was the reply.

Now, I ask you! How are you supposed to keep a straight face when all you can envision is the concentration that must have been involved for this boy to urinate into the tiny opening of a water pistol? I took a sudden coughing fit and dashed into the outer office, followed by the phys. ed. teacher who demanded that I sentence Jamie to an appropriate punishment. Eventually, I condemned him to an incarceration period of one hour, so that he could wash down the walls and floors of the boys' change room. I don't think that phys. ed. teacher has forgiven me yet. I'm really not able to perform under pressure!

I had to deal with another young man who was brought into the office for fighting in the playground. At eight years old, he stood three foot nothing, and yet he had managed to pound the daylights out of a ten-year-old of considerably greater weight and height. To make matters worse, I swear this kid has been christened Rocky.

"Well, Rocky, I hear you've been fighting," says I. "Do you know the punishment for fighting in the playground, Rocky?"

"Yes, Mrs. Baker. You get the strap."

"Right, Rocky. Since you know the punishment, could you tell me why you started a fight? Do you want to be a boxer when you grow up, Rocky?" says I, a great believer in sarcasm.

"That's right, Mrs. Baker!" he excitedly exclaimed. "I had to get some practice in!" Again, abject failure! I collapsed in a giggling heap. I eventually made Rocky promise he'd never again fight at school and let him go. He kept his promise for two whole years, which I thought was pretty good.

The teacher on outside duty approached me one day to say she was going to bring Doug to me for heaving an empty can at a classmate

and causing a small cut on his head. I was mentally prepared for the encounter and figured I would have no difficulty in dealing with the case with the sternness it deserved.

Enter teacher and student.

"Well, Mrs. Allen, do we have some problem here?" I enquired.

"I'm sure you realize that Doug has been in several scrapes this year, Mrs. Baker," responded the teacher. "But today's episode we simply can't ignore."

"Maybe you'd better explain exactly what happened, Doug," I said.

"Well, Mrs. Baker, it was like this. I got mad at Danny and I picked up this kin tan — I mean tin can, and I heaved the kin tan — I mean tin can, at him and the kin tan — I mean tin can, cut him on the head."

By this time both the teacher and I were edging out the door. We ran down the hallway and, between fits of laughter, yelled "Tin can" and "Kin tan" at each other. I eventually sobered up enough to sentence Doug to two recesses with his nose pressed against the office wall.

Who Is the Teacher's Pet?

On the first day of the fall term, I often set my class the job of writing a story about themselves as their introduction to me. I assign this task because the result can tell a great deal about the students, who are writing what they regard as the essential information about themselves. One girl summed herself up with the words: "Im elivin year's old and Im big and fat." Right about then, you decide that if she never learns to multiply in your class you couldn't care less. You certainly hope, though, that you'll be able to convince her that she's a person of some worth. Another student stated that his mom and dad like him O.K. but they *really* like his baby sister. They told their friends all the funny things she did, but they never told anybody about the things he did, although he's even drawn them pictures. Another little fellow told me he'd tried out for hockey last winter but didn't make the team. He figured he'd try again this fall, but he sure hoped his dad wouldn't yell at him the way he did last year.

Who is the teacher's pet? Children will ponder this question and decide that, given the evidence of the teacher's words and actions, X must be the teacher's pet; if not X, then Y surely is the one. When students try to entice their teacher into naming the pet, the teacher invariably states that he or she doesn't have one. Most of the time, this is a bald-faced lie. But if the teacher did admit to having a pet, the students would never believe the person named is *really* the teacher's pet. The teacher's pet is not the one that the teacher never yells at. The teacher's pet is not the bold student who dares to play tricks on the teacher and provokes laughter. The teacher's pet is not the student who consistently gets the highest marks. The teacher's pet is not the student who always studies for tests.

The teacher's pet is more likely to be that shy little girl who sits in the back and blushes when she's called upon to answer a question. The teacher's pet can be that fellow who's "never out of the office" because of his behaviour on the playground. The teacher's pet may well be the overweight girl who thinks she's ugly. The teacher's pet may be the lad who produces written work of average quality but betrays his acute intelligence in oral discussion groups. A teacher prizes such children for the most selfish of reasons: they have the potential to make a teacher feel that teaching is worthwhile. *If* the shy girl gains confidence, the troublemaker learns to count to ten before he swings at someone, the heavy girl starts to feel good about herself after she's been complimented on her dress a few times, and the underachiever gets his teeth into something that challenges him, *then* the teacher feels good and thinks, "Maybe I do deserve an apple for the teacher."

110